A GRAVE MISTAKE

By

James William Christenson

Kayto & Co. Publishing

Minneapolis | Minnesota | USA

A Grave Mistake

8860 154th Street West
Prior Lake, Minnesota, 55372

ISBN-13: 978-1-7375276-1-9

Library of Congress Control Number: 2021913771

THIS BOOK BELONGS TO:

DEAD-ICATION

Thanks to my family for all the free advice and encouragement.

Thanks to my parents who "only have twenty years left... and not even twenty good years," and especially to my father for all the wordsmithing.

~To those who are offended or disturbed by the nature of this tale: I completely agree with you. Stories about death aren't funny... unless they are executed properly.

A BRIEF NOTE TO THE READER

In the 1800s, bodysnatching was a rather common problem. Medical schools in earlier days received their cadavers for dissection from executions, and, other than those designated criminals, the dissection of the human form was illegal. As capital punishment became less frequent, institutions had fewer and fewer bodies for their students. In response, a vile but most lucrative business was formed. Previously, grave robbery could be profitable only if the body had been buried with jewelry, such as with the pharaohs of old, but with an increased demand for cadavers, a corpse could be worth much more than the items with which the dead was buried. Many petty crooks participated in the trafficking of the dead as the risk was rather low and the reward far higher. In the United Kingdom as well as the United States, bodysnatching was only a misdemeanor and punishable by a fine. However, the going rate was roughly $80 per corpse; a high dollar amount considering the average day laborer only earned approximately 16¢ per hour at the time. Graveyards across the United Kingdom and United States began hiring armed guards and erecting fences to stop this appalling business, but the reward was just too enticing. In 1896, an invention by the name of "The Coffin Torpedo" was put on the market to discourage resurrectors. This device would explode if the lid were ever lifted on a coffin after it had been sealed, leaving more than one body in its wake. Many superstitions hung over graveyards and the dead in general, which made for some interesting stories and discouraged quite a few from grave robbery. In this short story, several of these common beliefs are mentioned, and, as strange as they sound, many people believed them and some still do today. Please enjoy the slightly disturbed humor of… **A Grave Mistake.**

A timid rap at the door broke the priest's concentration. Hesitantly, a man entered wearing a brown tweed suit.

"Father, I'm sorry, but I cannot continue in my position," the groundskeeper said, wringing his hands nervously, the brim of his hat getting roughly maimed in the process. Beads of sweat dotted his furrowed brow and great purple bags pulled mercilessly at his bottom eyelids. His eyes darted nervously towards the window that overlooked the small parish graveyard, and his dry tongue incessantly attempted to wet his lips.

"Cyrus!" the priest exclaimed, looking up from the reading on his desk and noting what a state the poor groundskeeper was in. "What's the matter? You look as if you've seen a ghost." Cyrus shivered at this last remark. "And why this sudden decision to leave your job?"

"Well Father, I… um… I have conducted myself in a manner that seems to me grounds to resign." He drew a shaky arm across his forehead.

"Oh?" The priest looked at him with some confusion. "Please, have a seat."

Cyrus glanced out the window once more and the conflict of whether to take a seat or simply run out of the room was evident on his face. With a determined movement, Cyrus pulled a chair around and fell onto it as rigid as a board.

"Now, I want you to take a deep breath and tell me everything," the priest said with such a comforting tone in his voice that Cyrus's shoulders relaxed somewhat. Cyrus swallowed hard and began to recall the events that led to his resignation.

"The groundskeeper said, ringing his hands nervously..."

"Never known such a disrespectful display of negligence..."

"Well sir," he began, "it all started with my own pride. As you know, we've had a series of misfortunes at the parish. First, Chester Cromwell passed and was buried in his plot in the yard. It was a lovely service, and I thought I had done a brilliant job of making the grounds look proper, but the next day I was called on by a most distressed Mrs. Cromwell.

I opened the door and was near knocked over by the fury of the sobs and curses that poured out of her mouth. She said how she 'had never known such a disrespectful display of negligence in all her days," and as you know, that is quite a few days. Well, I was fairly wounded at these remarks, as I had no earthly idea what she was talking about. After Widow Cromwell finished her outburst and left, I sat for a moment in stunned incredulity and confusion.

After I regained my senses, I quickly donned my jacket and headed to the graveyard to investigate what had brought on her tirade. To my horror, when I arrived, I saw what had caused the widow's distress, and I nearly had a similar reaction! Mr. Cromwell's plot, may he rest in peace, was in complete disarray. The dirt was mounded at the side of the site, his coffin lay ajar, and the once neatly arranged flowers were strewn about the yard. Grave robbers had violated his resting place.

As you know, not three weeks later, poor Mrs. Cromwell joined her husband, and I was greeted at my door the day after the service by the family and received a reprimand so strong I feared for my safety. Sure enough, the same thing had happened. Grave robbers had desecrated her grave! I was filled with such a fury that I nearly broke my walking stick against the big oak. Then we had two more tragedies ending in the same result.

I was beginning to receive cold glances around the town and rumors began to spread defaming the parish and my work, so I devised a plan. It was an awful plan I now realize, and I have reaped a myriad of consequences for it. I haven't slept for two days and the little sleep I have gotten is haunted by the hellish features I have seen as a result of my scheme."

The priest's eyes grew wide and the manuscript he was reading fell from his hand as he scooted his chair a bit closer to Cyrus.

"Raymond Willard passed on, and after the service, when all had left, I sat with the coffin waiting for the gravediggers to finish digging the hole. My

thoughts began to wander, and let me tell you, Father, I have never understood the words 'idle hands make the devils work' quite so well until this incident. Anyways, I always get a bit of a queasy feeling when sitting with the departed. So, to distract myself, I was considering the homily you gave on Ezekiel's valley of dry bones, when a truly grotesque thought occurred to me: How terrible would it be if the body suddenly jumped out of the casket and began to chase me around the room?

That thought made me shudder, and I was going to put such foolish things from my mind when another, far more sinister, thought came to me. If such a thing didn't scare me to death, it certainly would discourage me from coming back to this parish, or any other for that matter. I knew that if these resurrection men had such a fright as a dead man springing to life and chasing them, they would certainly give up their sinful ways for good and leave our parish be. I debated with myself for quite some time trying to dissuade myself of the idea, but ultimately, I convinced myself of its merit. I would be buried instead of Raymond and give the robbers the worst scare of their lives. And so, I began to plan the details of my macabre task."

"Cyrus! You didn't!" the priest exclaimed in horror, a rather pallid color replacing his once plush cheeks. Cyrus closed his eyes and nodded most gravely. The priest crossed himself, momentarily glancing towards heaven. After a brief pause, Cyrus continued.

"As you know, Raymond had no family, so he had no graveside service, and being a rather wealthy man, he seemed to me a reasonably appealing target. He was the perfect fit for my plan. All I needed was someone to help me stash the body temporarily and dig me up if the robbers failed to strike. "Only one other soul should know about my plan to rid the parish once and for all of these bodysnatchers," I thought to myself.

Unfortunately for poor Douglas Hammond, he was loitering in the churchyard at the time and became my reluctant accomplice. At first, he strongly protested my idea, but with enough pressure he gave in, and soon enough we had removed Raymond and stowed him in the vestry.

This was not a simple chore, and I am ashamed at the lack of delicacy in how this task was performed. We had the most difficult time extracting him from the box. He simply wouldn't come out. Every time we tried to lift him, the box came up with him. We weren't sure why he wasn't coming out of the casket, so we lowered the box to the floor, and I anchored my foot on the side of the frame.

With one final wrench, Raymond came flying out of the coffin and both Douglas and I fell backwards. The stiff figure fell full upon Douglas, and Doug let out a shriek that made me likewise holler in fright. Once we had regained our nerve, we assessed the situation. The reason Raymond's body was not easily removed was due to the fact that he had died with both arms outstretched and they

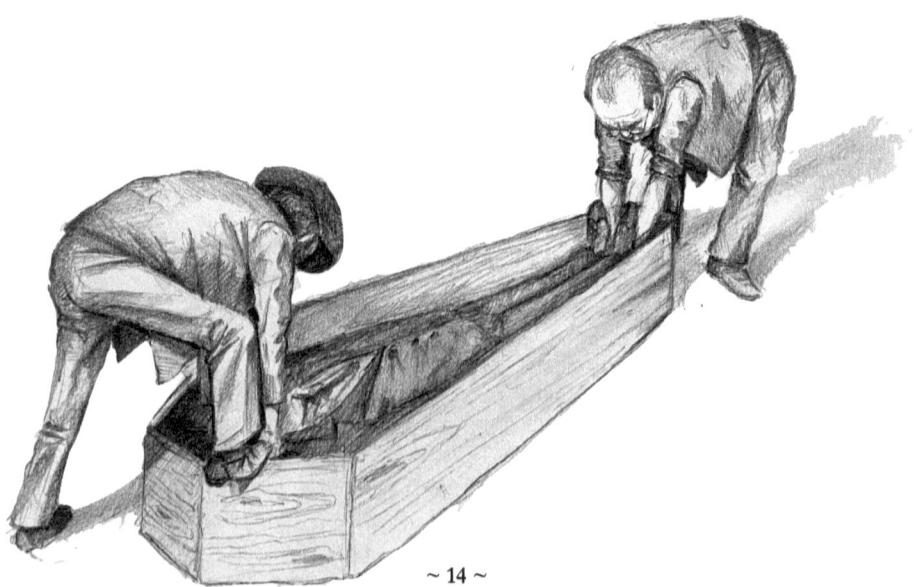

had stiffened that way so he appeared as a 'T.' Those who had placed him in his casket had fastened his arms to his side in order to get him in. When we loosed him from his box his arms came free. This caused more problems than we had anticipated.

Fitting him through the small door of the vestry now was the next obstacle to overcome. I took the upper body, and Douglas, being the smaller, took the feet. However, Raymond's stiff physique refused to yield and with his odd form of extended arms, we couldn't maneuver him very well. Douglas managed to fit his portion through the narrow doorway, but my portion didn't slide through as easily, and our first attempt ended in us dropping him to the hard wood floor, and he landed face down upon it. I turned the body over and jumped back about five feet screaming all the way. The stitching had broke on his eyes, and they had sprung open. Poor Douglas was trapped in the small vestry with the corpse blocking the aperture and gaping at him with his yellow, blink-less gaze.

Not quite knowing what to do, and shrieking in alarm, he ran back and forth between the walls of the room in desperation, looking for an escape.

After I mollified the quivering Douglas, we attempted the feat once more, this time tipping the corpse to his side, but this made my already precarious grip far worse, and we had a similar result on our second attempt. I suggested breaking the fellow's arms for an easier go of things, but Douglas heaved at the very notion, and I dropped the matter quickly as I saw that his already tenuous mental state would've just shattered.

Our third attempt ended successfully, and we took a moment to consider the events of the last thirty or so minutes. Douglas looked positively ill. His mouth hung open, he was breathing hard, and his complexion matched that of the man we had just stuffed in the vestry."

The priest glanced towards the vestry door with a frown of disapproval, and Cyrus continued his account.

"Well, we headed back to where we had left the coffin and conscious of the inherent dangers of my proposed adventure, I put into place a few bodily precautions. I drilled a small hole through the side of the coffin to provide an air source until I was placed in the ground and placed a canteen of water at the head of the casket. Then I, myself, filled the vacant coffin.

Douglas replaced the lid, and aside from the thin beam of light that filtered through the seam, all was dark. My confidence in my decision began to waver as the closeness of the tomb enabled me to feel the warmth of my breath, and a feeling of being trapped settled in. A great thwack shook the whole coffin as Douglas drove the first nail in through the lid, and my feeling of claustrophobia increased greatly. I was about to shout to Douglas to free me, but I refrained, and reaffirmed my anger at the robbers, and so took several breaths to calm myself.

As the minutes passed, my anxiety diminished a bit, but my discomfort did not. My nose itched, the useless canteen leaned against my head, and there was not enough space to slide my arm up to my face. This discovery induced another wave of panic, but I soothed myself by thinking how delightful it would be to scare those robbers. However, as the temperature in the coffin rose, the box reeked ever more strongly of the somewhat poorly preserved previous inhabitant, and the odor became so noxious I didn't want to breathe. I forgot my discomfort when I heard muffled voices and the slam of the church door. The next thing I knew I was being lifted

"The stiff figure fell full upon Douglas..."

roughly about and couldn't help listening to the ghastly conversation between the gravediggers.

'I don't know why we even bother to bury 'em! Them robbers will just undo all of our work,' a gruff voice said.

'Ha! You think thems are robbers that's been overturnin' them gravesites? That ain't no robbers' handiwork.'

The second voice was much more nasally, and a short pause occurred after this comment.

'Well?' the gruff voice questioned.

'Whatdya mean 'well'?' said the other.

'Who's been bodysnatchin' if it warn't robbers?'

I was now greatly intrigued by these fellows' conversation and more than a bit concerned. I had never before considered that my theory of grave robbers might be wrong.

'Why, the old horned man himself!' the nasally one finished, and with that, my stomach flew into my mouth as the casket was unceremoniously dropped into the hole. The coffin crashed to the earth, and I let out a yelp upon impact.

'What was that?' the gruff voice near shouted.

'Not sure! But it's bad luck to listen to the spirits so we'se best get diggin' and get out of here!'

The thud of dirt covering the lid heightened my unease with each percussive thump, and I winced at every shovelful.

'Ya know, the old man wasn't taken out of his house feet first, which means a family member of his is gunna die tonight or tomorrow!' continued the gruff voice, now just breaking through the rhythmic thud of the dirt.

'Good thing the old coot didn't have no family,' the other replied between scoops.

'Oh, that means who'sever touched the body last is gunna be the one who kicks the bucket. And that won't be no perdy way to go, neither!' the gruff one continued.

The other man whistled in astonishment. At this I began racking my brain trying to remember if it were I or Douglas who had last touched the body. I didn't exactly believe these fellows, but their dialogue was so fervent that it was hard not to wonder if they weren't on to something.

'Heavens! Now you've done it! The Devil is a-comin'! Dan't you know nothin'? Never whistle in a graveyard. It summons the Devil and he takes who'sever is nearest 'ta Hell with him when he comes, body and soul!'

'Well, since I'm taller than you, I'm closer to Heaven, which means he's gunna get you.'

Little did they know that there was one closer in proximity to Hell than both of them and that they were sealing him into his grim fate. This thought disturbed me further, and I wanted to let out a holler to notify them of my presence and have them help me escape my tomb. If only I had, but my own pride at the perfection of my plan stayed my voice.

The gravediggers' discourse became more and more muffled as the dirt weighed down more heavily upon the roof of the casket.

Bit by bit the poorly constructed casket bowed and the satin lining pressed down upon my chest!

'Hurry up! I don't want to incite anymore misfortune than you've already brought on us in this unholy place! For Pete's sake, if I saw a black cat today, I'd know for certain I was done for.'

That was the last clear statement I could make out before all the voices were just a low hum above me. Had I seen a black cat that day? I thought I might've. I begun to panic as the very walls of the coffin seemed to compress me, squeezing the air right out of my lungs. Horrific images flashed in my mind of ghoulish demons dragging me downwards into the open mouth of Hell.

The air in the coffin was becoming moist and hot with my own perspiration and breath. How much air did I have left, I wondered, as each breath seemed to satiate me less and less. I began to press against the sides of my sepulcher and screamed as my arms met only resistance each way they turned. My only hope remained in Douglas.

Then a thought sent my mind into utter pandemonium. If Douglas touched the body last, he would die tonight, and no one would recover me, aside from the Devil himself! I'm not sure how much time passed while I struggled to wriggle my way free of the nightmare I was in, but it felt as if time was moving as slow as molasses itself.

My screams stopped as did my heart when I heard, or felt rather, through the ground, a subtle vibration, and then another.

The vibrations increased in volume until I recognized them as unnatural footfalls from above. Could these footsteps be made by hooves instead of human feet, I wondered?

Now my mind was screaming but my body was completely paralyzed in terror. Then I heard a devilish spade striking the earth! I had no crucifix, no holy relic with which I could repel the foul creatures coming for my body and soul. As the shovel drew nearer, I could hear low, wicked laughter. The laughter sent a chill scurrying down my spine.

The digging instrument struck the top of the coffin with a horrid screech. As the dirt was scraped from the roof of my trap, I could hear a low hiss as if a lantern were burning. I could only assume it was the hellish brimstone trailing the creatures. I felt the coffin uprooted from the pit, lifted up, and dropped upon the ground above.

A metal probe splintered through the lid and I saw through the crack a horrid orangish glow! The lid, with a dreadful creak, gave way and flew off.

Three monstrous figures stood over me, illuminated by some unseen fire below. The first had a great scar running from his lip up to his milky white eye. The second and largest of the trio wore a grin that shined out from under a great beard in the orange glow, and the third was especially scrawny with the largest noses I had ever seen. His nostrils flared and a puff of smoke poured forth from them.

"I stumbled into Vernon's pond..."

I screamed the most blood curdling scream I have ever released. To this day my voice is still hoarse. Quick as I could I jumped from the casket and ran blindly into the blackened night. I didn't stop running or screaming until I stumbled into Vernon's Pond behind the parish. It is only by God's grace that I still walk this earth, for I am sure that those demons were after me."

The priest sat absolutely stunned by the account he had just heard. In all his days as a priest, he had never witnessed such an incredible and horrific tale.

"And so… as you can see, I can no longer remain in my position at this establishment and am, in fact, considering moving to another town."

"Cyrus…" The priest searched for something to say. "I don't even have the words. Do what you must, and God be with you," he finally managed.

Cyrus nodded, mumbled a thanks, and exited the small building.

The priest sat, not just a little bewildered, unable to go back to his reading. He spent quite a considerable time staring out the window with a puzzled look upon his face. A knock at the parish door broke his trance. He stood, traversed the floor, and opened the door.

Three men stood in the entryway. They looked haggard and greatly distressed. One was an incredibly large man with an unkempt beard. The one directly behind him had a great scar that ran the full length of his face and a bad eye with a milky white film. The third was rather thin and wore a scowl under his inordinately large nose. A pipe hung from his lips and a spiral of smoke escaped his nostrils.

"Parson... uh... er... I mean Rev'rend... er, whatever...Um, we've got some 'fessin' up to do," said the largest. "You see, we don't 'xactly make our wages in an honorable fashion. Well, I should say 'didn't'. We was bodysnatchers, and we made our bread pilferin' graves and selling cadavers to medical institutions. But the events of two nights ago have set us on the straig't and narra' quicker than a hobo suckin' down mash. We was about to dig up that thar grave, and we was all in great spirits, having just dined like kings and drunk like blaggards. Joe set the lantern down on the ground and we got to work unearthin'.

"Joe set the lantern down..."

We was tryin' to be quiet about things but, being a bit soused, we found our task to be funny for some reason and begun a-laughin'. Gunther shagged after us, sayin' how God would judge us for laughing at our wickedness, but I says, 'If God cared for the dead, he'd send 'em back to stop us.' We had a few more laughs before our spades struck the coffin. We cleared the dirt and hoisted the thing out in front of our lantern. I took my crowbar and begun to pry the lid. The lid flew off and reveal'd a fine specimen. Why, he hardly even looked dead! Just then, the body come to life and screeched somethin' awful. We in turn howled in terror. The thing sprung from its casing and begun to chase us, a-screamin' and a-shriekin' all the while! Joe fainted and Gunth and I headed for the hills.

We didn't stop 'till we was convinced the creature was gone for good. We warn't sure if it had gotten Joe, and we debated whether or not to go back and collect his remains. We snuck back and found the yard empty. No sign of the foul thing. It almost made things worse not knowing where it had got to."

The two men behind the speaker began to get a bit fidgety, and their gazes floated around the yard, nervously scrutinizing every bit of movement.

"We darted into the yard, shook Joe to life, and like that, we was gone. After havin' no sleep for a good while we decided to seek some heavn'ly advice and repent of our ways. Boy, I'll sure as hell never test God with my words long as I live!"

"The thing sprung from its casing..."

The priest stood with tears in his eyes and a reddened face, a grimace on his quivering lips. The ruffians assumed it was due to their tale of horror.

The parish door shut behind three newly christened believers. The priest returned to his desk, a smile plastered across his face. "I shall prepare the elements for tomorrows' service," thought he as he walked to the vestry to retrieve the necessary items.

The three reformed resurrection men swore they heard one last scream from that horrid creature coming from behind the parish and quickened their pace down the road.

THE END

"...Heard one last scream from that horrid creature..."

THANKS!

I'd like to personally thank you for reading my book. It is my sincere hope you throughly enjoyed it - I had tremendous fun writing and illustrating it!

Would you please consider leaving feedback, particularly on Amazon.com or your bookseller of choice? I would greatly appreciate it! Your reviews make this book more visible and less buried (pun intended) for those who might not otherwise discover it. Your thoughts would be more than usually valued. Thanks again!

www.JamesWilliamArt.com

www.ingramcontent.com/pod-product-compliance
Lightning Source LLC
Chambersburg PA
CBHW050907180626
46814CB00007B/2934